JUST OFFSIDE

ABHIN THULASIDAS

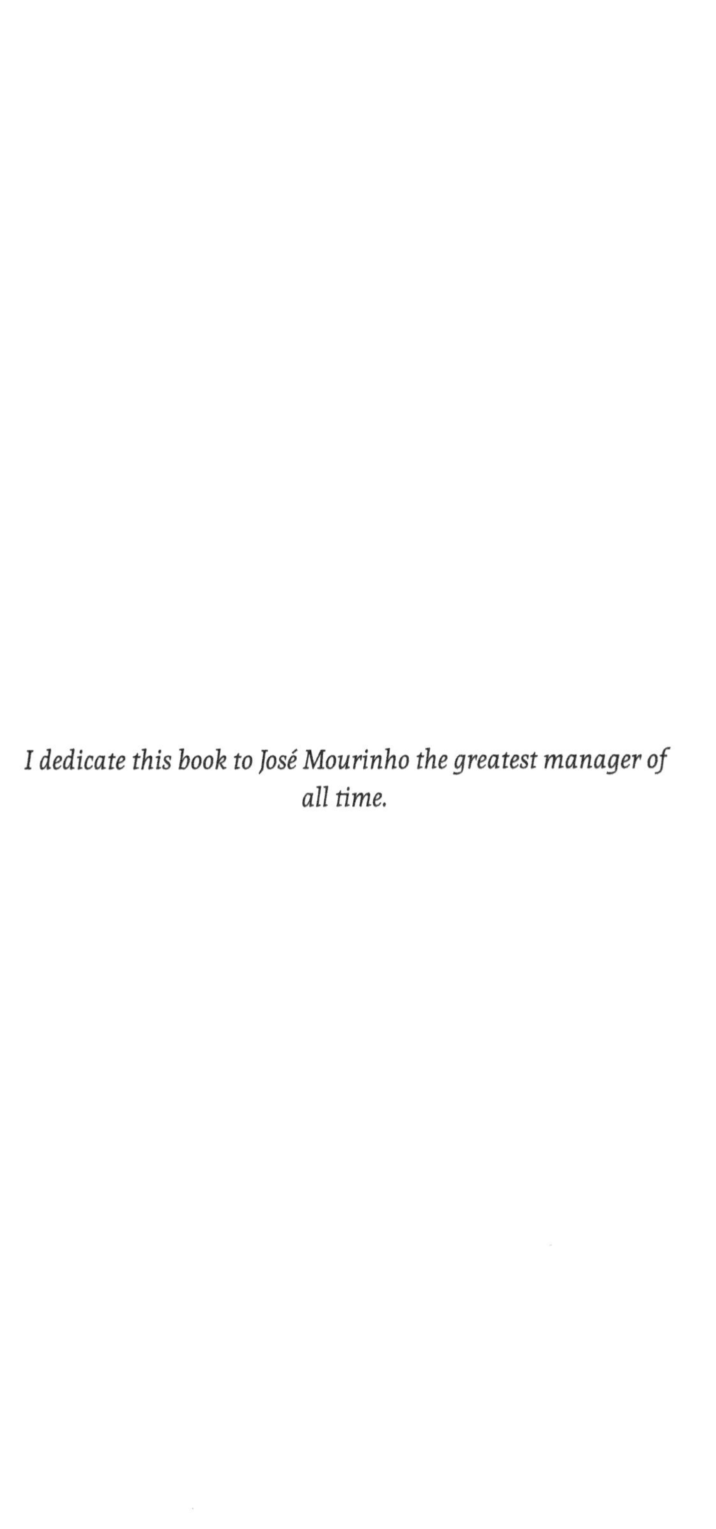

I dedicate this book to José Mourinho the greatest manager of all time.

Contents

Preface

Many haven't achieved what you did
Yet the hate often unbearable
Maybe it's just defaming acts
or it's your own success
What it matters for others is defeats
Foes born of jealousy surplus,
But they are never capable
And never will achieve what you did

You hath inspired football world
Into believing that anything is possible
Even in this pay to win era....
Bald frauds might try to seize your throne
But they won't even come close
You will never have a clone
You hath achieved the impossible
And it will be remembered till the end of the world

If not this rhyme shall....

Acknowledgements

Albeit they may seem impossible, I thank myself for never giving up on my dreams.

Prologue

Probably the most anticipated football match of the decade.Monaco taking on the mighty Munich.The underdogs holding onto a shaky one nil lead.

"They might have a chance to break here..."

"That's a lovely ball through to Enza"

"And it's a goaaal goaaaaaaa....."

"Who else ? It's the wonderkid Enza Gaeton and Monaco are through to the champions league semi final"

"Is this a dream Peter?"

"Well this is what dreams are made of"

Some kid from a spring fair,
Let go off a helium balloon;
It's flying very very far away....
Into the blue white sky -
Now it's gone so far far away
Altitude made it seen by -
All n ol' saw even those from the blue moon,
As it rose made blossom by the red glare.

Several big clubs including United are eyeing to sign the 21 year old French superstar Enza Gaeton. Several reports claimed that United had already made a bid of 90 million for the young forward.

Like almost all other stars -
This one too rose from humble beginnings.
Route was hard but he never felt it tough.
Each drop of sweat from hard work is sweet,
Sweetest is sweet but never sweet enough.
As cocoons hid in green discreet -
But rose with beautiful wings,
He lit like adorned altars.

As misty glasses covering eyes;

Hard work to paid work developed.
Virtual worship nurtured new found ego
But as night bugs never seen....
But that annoying noise far go.
Still hideout in the dark left them unseen,
As virtual world is where many thrive undetected.
They formed a new world hid from social eyes.

Once fraid of favor -
Now around alike flies around light,
Whether the glow dim they may flee..
To another bright to another...
As they are blinded floating looking for glee,
As a drunken man ever been sober.
Those that ol' brought by height -
Last until a thrown ball fall over.

Can Enza Gaeton carry a struggling United side?

Aging players with no replacement,
Clueless board spending on twigs
And managers sacked in quick cycles.
Once table toppers now stuck mid table -
Newly adopted clubs raised even more obstacles
But the most betted horse has had come at the new stable.
Dressing room stunned ! even the prized pigs -
Fans excited, showered positive comments

First game for the rookie
Similar a newborn peeps it's beak out;
From the shell...
He was subbed on at half time.
Provided an assist but his team did fail -

To yet another draw as recent regime,
But the youngster made a shout out;
That has had a sweet filled cookie.

The dressing room is a burning furnace;
Flamed by defeat, cooled by victory.
Players acting rash after loss....
Coaches feeling more n more pressure...
Then the disappointed fans blamed the boss.
The following game was an away fixture,
If that one too ends in failure, coach would be history
As big spending owners wrinkled their face

*United coach Van Der Sans dropped under enormous pressure
as his side has now lost three games in a row.*

As a carbonated drink bottle,
When shook the bubbles fizz up
Thus such was the pressure
Manager ready for the sack;
And also for the treasure...
A mid season sack costs the club back,
These days patience have no scope
As patience often is essential but it matters little.

*Yet another United manager has been sacked.
Jose Santos Felix was the next in line for the throne. Fans were
excited as the new coach was announced who had over twenty
titles in his name.*

Man is delighted by the thirst for change,
More delightful est to witness someone fail...
In a blink of an eye thousands are born;

That delight for many.
As thousands are reborn -
Sorrow of parting for many.
The fall of one shall -
Be the rise for another, c'est not strange.

Pundits doubted the new recruit...
Some fans were still uncertain,
Players were ready for a quick reboot
Gaffer and his staff punctual -
For the first training pursuit
But it was a formal greeting ritual
Unnecessary rather profane
Who knows what hides behind a suit?

The reporters sniffed the smell,
The first press conference...
They aimed poisoned darts at him,
Mostly about previous sackings -
He defended it with an adopted smile yet dim,
Which seemed like arrogant stings.
Either way all felt his presence -
Internet flooded with trolls and more troll

First few games were a blast...
Team scored a lot n lots of goals
And conceded just few,
But those were relatively weaker opponents,
Tougher challenges rallied next in queue
Defensive errors and letting in late goals were worrying
trends -
Which was a result of cheap free kicks and fouls.
He scratched his head to fixit fast

Training brings out talent and expose attitude
Astonishing how much an athlete trains !
Premier league being very physical;
Gaffer advised the rookie to adapt quick -
For extra fitness and to make his finishing clinical
But his attitude was kinda real sick
He jogged as people in a highway lane,
Forcing the manager to intrude...

More the fortune faster it drains
Of course the hunger and motivation -

*After a hectic week involving a champions league away fixture
players were given a quick breather.
But Jose made it sure that the players were assigned to
additional training during off days.*

Few players started a rebellion;
They skipped the training;
That very eve met at a cozy place
A party at team mates tiny little mansion.
Liquor and women plenty to trace.
Half the team present at the occasion
Such that a fowl spend spooning
They shared drinks with their single night union

Even the strongest man,
Easily overcome by lust.
Even the wisest,
Tempted by pleasure
All have it kept closed in mind's closet...
Can't blame a teenager's burning desire.

Whenst age catch up such that iron rust,
That too fade then -

Jose being furious with the players, benched even the superstars in the following game.
The game up against Palace turned out to be a huge disaster.....4-2 defeat at old clifftop. And the international break made it even more worse.

Football once was a beautiful game
When players played for the badge,
Nowadays just a profession
Blessed with a hefty paycheck.
There's a lack of passion
Such sick attitude brings stick;
Mostly from annoyed fans on those in charge
That for modern football is a shame

Duty becomes a job without passion,
A job becomes a devotion with commitment.
No one would dream to be stuck in an office chair;
But that is the unwanted destiny for many.
Such fate never unfair -
For who never dreamt of any
Big dreams often bring big disappointment,
Though even in defeat pride is the emotion

Diego Lorente was one of the senior pros in the team. His controversial press conference created a rift in the dressing room.

"I came here to regain my fitness...
My plan is to go back to Real

My plan was always to go to a small club
And regain my match fitness.
But I am loyal to the club
My intend is to aim high never less...
Hard work is always there
I want to get back to the top"

Lorente was on loan from Madrid. But his disrespect for United enraged the fans as well as the manager.

Jose's press conference before the Manchester derby was a blast.

"Let's talk about loyalty
Such a man can't be loyal to his wife
I'm not worried about
Of course he's not our player
I prefer not to comment on him,
But this club made great fortune for him
I zink some players want to be on the bench
They hate the football pitch"

No wonder Jose was fuming at Lorente. Jose escorted Lorente to the bench for the rest of his loan spell. Lorente's absence became an opportunity for Gaeton as he was the only natural replacement. Thus more time on the pitch for the youngster.

The season was almost over,
Reason at most lower
Players most ate all drained
Like the almighty took a rest on the Seventh day,
This break they have achieved
After a heating dismay -
Few players went under cover...

Others back to family hour....

This season is finished.

But the Gaffer's job ain't done yet
He had to look for reinforcements...
New summer signings
Few kids from the academy
Plus the recruitment team findings.
To sharpen the attack and a defensive remedy
Bargain is what trade laments -
Now it's upto the chairman to set...

ᚦᚦᚦ

"Rumor float that you're leaving Paris.
Is there any truth in these speculations ?"

The half wit interviewer questioned Luka Ivanovic.

"I know when to stay when to leave
Rest can simply shut up....
Rumors are my girls
They smear about such matter
Luka send my naughty fowls
To spread my chatter
Who he knows often stay silent
Silence thus is my reply."

Jose was aware of Luka's contract situation and made a phone call to persuade him to join United.

"Ola!"

"Not many trespassers dare to call Luka"

"As you already know I'm at United
I know your future is at cross roads
Right time to choose only come once
I want you here.
You have much more to offer
Our ambitions are always the same
They will never change either
You come here and let's win together...."

"You're a prick mister
Remember you benched me
Cause of a damn party
Not falling for an old flame trying to reconnect
I haven't made my decision yet
But very unlikely
Not a chance...not at all
Better no hope than false hope"

"I'm not your girl trying to reconnect
Who you caught cheating
Remember that season you had under me
I made you one of the best
You were the main man for me
I can't motivate rocks and make them fly
But I zink I have chance with you
Never be quick to make a choice..."

"Hard work is my synonym
I made myself
Don't expect me to join your club
There are plenty of them chasing me
Just like those Instagram models
Good try old man
But I don't keep any grudge against you
Not anymore I guess."

Most clubs are run by businessmen
Most owners lack the vision;
Glasses help you see -
But doesn't help your eyes
Owners ignore fan's plea,
They work under a disguise
Like a tortoise beneath its den

United chief McCain Edwood contacts Luka Ivanovic' agent.

"We have interest for one of your clients
Sure rumors reached your ear
Our past inclinations dive deep
This one a very likely deal.
Let's put our conscience to sleep
And make a filthy deal
Now stop other clubs move from rear
I expect your best compliments"

Rino Fiola replies after a delayed pause.

"My clients are of giant stature
Contracts will be with no loop holes

Would also add few clauses
Least important is his opinion
Him either not so fond of English places
Hams and Leys don't please him to stay on -
Anyway I may ask his calls
My agent fee though will rapture"

And finally a possible signing after the Gaffer's relentless
pressure. But Jose wasn't happy as he wanted to add few more
players to strengthen the squad.
But McCain Edwood ain't the type that could be squeezed.

"Stop the moaning already lad
We are on the verge of a super signing
Now focus on your job
Which is still on a cliff
A slight slip and you can sob
Imagine her leaving before bob gets stiff
You man better get running
And don't make me mad"

Jose almost lost his cool again.

"What about the centre back
We need one desperately
Nothing wrong with current defenders
Except they don't know how to defend...
We lack true leaders in the team
We need more players with winning mentality
Otherwise we couldn't achieve what we aim for,
I zink we need to complete the puzzle"
"Out you go old man
No more signings this window.

You got my sympathy as to a beggar
A craftsman works with what he has
Don't get the things foggier
Stop moaning like a miser cass
Temme what I didn't know
About this squad mahn"

"But I might consider signing someone from.....the farmer's
league"

In some leagues, there are only one or two big teams.
They win the title every year
They are like and more like landlords -
Rest of the teams are farmers
They cultivate new talents
The big teams shamelessly buy ol' the good players,
Even hijack managers...
Thus they win the league every year with zero competition.

However, the farmer's leagues produce some of the finest young
players with great potential.

There's no water in the land,
Just a few muddy patches in water.
A glass of beer doesn't make you drunk -
But a bad comment could make you act drunken
Even the most skillful slightly sunk,
When more eyes concentrate causing a burden
Even if talent is your daughter,
If hard work is your prodigal son bothe doesn't stand.

United's troubles never seemed this disastrous at first. More
voids appeared every passing minute.

But Luka Ivanovic's signing has been made official.

"I joined this club to win trophies
The choice made after one thought
This club is rich in heritage
I won a lot before here
But my desire to win still remains constant
I hope the opposition defenders are ready
They might have had nightmares
I torture them and throw them to transfer lobbies "

Earth is more flat than round
Yet no man will conquer ol' the places in part.
Football has another world innit -
It's a religion to many
A million are faithful devotees of it
Gods, idols and legends so many
Passion makes it more than a sport;
That little lantern amongst the largest crowd

Meanwhile, some of Jose's comments made young Gaeton furious. Jose claimed in a post match press conference that he was not giving his best every game.

C'est a shame not all with wings can fly...
Some have egos bigger than their future
Passion and desire help you run faster
Lack of it just slows you down.
Some use harsh words to rise higher
Others make grudge and drag themselves down.
Those that man up and self nurture
And the rest finding ways to never try....

Enza and Ledley who were one of the players from the academy planned an outing.

Everyone stared at the lad -
As if he just landed from the Jupiter
It was really annoying.
His buddy didn't intrude,
As he was used to the constant pestering
But the young star found it rude
He became red but not the later
As he was adjusted to this freak salad

Total strangers invading privacy,
Cheese faces with a phone
Trying to click a quick selfie
Celebs aren't just chick magnets
They also attract blind and pity;
For caught in fishing nets,
Strive to leave their life alone
Those caught in illusion makes it easy.

They went to a bar in disguise
Had a few drinks
Accidentally the cap worn as disguise fell off;
One or two noticed....
They tried to roam off,
But they quickly pounced -
Before a two winks
It was an effing disgrace !

Enza and Ledley were surrounded in the bar.

The enraged young man pushed them away
He wasn't aware that cameras were filming it !
It took some time for them to escape
Never such a hangout ever again.
Lucky they got out in good shape
Never never not ever again.
They rushed off from the street and took a bit
Then took their cars and dashed through the highway

*Someone posted Gaeton's rash behavior on the internet. It went
viral as everything except art conquers the internet.*

"Kid you are new in this league
You have no time to wander
Or to get in trouble.
Don't feed your distractions,
Your earnings if I am true are double now
But your efforts I have to question
But I can't question your talent
It's still in you and I can help you explode"

Jose advised Gaeton.

Pieces of Advice are the most annoying thing for youth.

ᚦᚦᚦ

They were more like bro n brother
And less like friends
Teammates since teenage,
They rose through the ranks
Now playing in the top tier stage

They were linked by numerous links
But their friendship just ended -
By betrayal that could make souls shatter.

Levy and Gibbs were prominent figures in the dressing room.

They went vibing together with their lovers
Lovely trip with them wives
A pleasant family hangout
Forming a ever present alliance;
Take the sweetest fruit with a pinch of salt,
Can't distinguish fraudulent lenience
If a human had nine lives -
Zis sins would be bigger than the universe...

As usual returning to his shelter...
Something suspicious as a car was parked outside
He was escorted in by pressure
As he noticed presence of someone in;
He heard and seen perfidious pleasure
Such a sight a real torture for the brain.
Like a stunning goal ruled out by offside,
The disappointment is just beyond better

Gibbs witnessed the most inhuman betrayal ever. Poetry has to be ruthless and clear.
Levy slept with his wife.

Ever since that incident, there was a growing discomfort. Several clashes even during the training sessions. Jose and his coaching staff tried their best to intercede. Levy was a goal scoring attacking midfield player. Very important part of the squad. Gibbs was just a second choice right back who could

*be easily replaced. Though Gibbs had a huge influence in the
dressing room.*

"No secrets here and it is no secret that..
Your girl has been passed around like a joint.
It is nothing that concerns me or my job
But the clashes in the dressing room....
You have to stay professional."

Jose was more than frank with Gibbs.

"Mister this club is my life
I have been playing here for so long
I never asked for playing time
Never bothered you about the defensive tactics
This is my club
I will put my personal life back home"

Some serious trust issues....
Loyalty is indeed a clever man's disguise.

"Trust me"

Said McCain Edwood.

"The problem is the defense guy
He's not very quick
Sloppy with his passes
Lazy in the training
He sponsored us many defeats -
Playing a liability isn't substantial gaining
You know the tricks
Deal with him sly.."

"I would love to see how you react
If you hear someone slept with your wife"

*In the following press conference, the journalists were sniffing
for blood.*

"Hi Jose ....There is footage of two members of your squad
almost quarreling."

"I zink.... I'm zinking... this club is zinking"

*Jose was aware of the situation. He couldn't bench levy. He was
one of United's better players if not the best. Being a manager
is tough. Jose had to choose between the most influential player
on the pitch against the most influential player in the dressing
room. Gibbs was benched causing a negative vibe in the dressing
room.*

Lands are divided by water -
Hearts are divided by guilt.
Lil bit of sugar destroys the hardest enamel...
Betrayal breaks the strongest bonds.
Distance is quite normal....
When two close people taunt
Easily broken but hardly built -
Just like a well played move disgraced by a sitter

The changing room divided,
Gaffer couldn't favor a side
Tried his best to stay impartial -
But rather forced to pick a side
As few contacts in speed dial,

Rest in the regular contacts slide.
If forced to divide,
Better each slice equally divided

The rift in the dressing room became clearly visible.

ᐅᐅᐅ

The training ground is an arena -
Where the warriors exhibit their skills.
Some fought with skill,
Some fought with strength,
Some worked harder beyond the training drill.
Others were lazy calculating the pitch width;
Football isn't just to pay the bills -
C'est about the passion and mana.

Injuries were roadblocks.
Never easy to replace some;
Can't replace salt with pepper
Key players are irreplaceable.
It was such a summer -
The team was unstable
Making cohesion rather tiresome,
Even the young players took few knocks

As half the players stopped playing for him
Few key players still injured
They results became worse.
Only positive was the league position
Fans voices were very hoarse...
They failed against tough opposition -
But kept the top four secured

Albeit the title challenge already dim

Inorder to fix the insane,
Gaffer added few extra training sprees
It was to solve few riots -
And to set a few principles
As to drag back flown kites,
Spinning the twine in circles
But sometimes the yarn breaks free....
C'est alike watering the crops after a rain.

The whole season was a disaster
But they still finished fifth,
And won a minor trophy
But it never pleased the fans....
The team was playing sloppy
They blamed the manager's defensive stance.
Success takes time -
Losing patience takes lesser time...

Ever since the plastic clubs emerged,
The competition became tighter -
As their owners threw cash.
There are few which can't be bought with money -
Like passion and fans never afforded.
Though their business grew healthier by the stash
Even with the half empty stadiums marked

2

The Fifa Worldcup approached closer. The most prestigious competition in the world of football.

Stage where new talents are born
Even underdogs stood a chance....
Fighting to make their nations proud,
Nothing less than the biggest festival in football
Voices enchanted by patriotism became loud
C'est spirit, c'est passion, c'est football !
Ol' cultures united at a glance -
Each determined to give all before the final whistle.

I got something to fight for
I got something to live for.....

But ol' I got is a million dreams
And a broken heart
There's no magic in my feet
But this fire in my heart -
Is glowing is glowing glowing glowing.....
When I walked past yesterday
All I saw was this door...

I got something to fight for

I got something to live for

Ol' I got is a million dreams
Ol' I have is a broken heart
And if I am true there's no magic in my feet
But this fire in my heart -
Is glowing is glowing glowing glowing.....

Now I got something to fight for
I got something to live for...

Even If this dream die
Even if the flames die
As the repelling breeze blew,
But it still kept shining
Kept shining shining shining

I have something to fight for
I have something to live for
Still growing still growing growing....

Io ho avuto qualcosa per cui lottere
Io ho avuto qualcosa per cui vivere...

Enza Gaeton played a key role in the world cup winning French national team. Soon he became one of the biggest superstars in world football.He was even nominated for the ballon d'or. An award which never made any sense anyway. More corrupt than anything else.

The new season was about to start.Enza picked up a minor injury. United fans expected Jose Santos Felix to steer them to a Premier league title.However the gaps weren't filled yet.

Once a man tried to walk to the moon
He challenged everything on his path -
Traveled at night and rested in the morning
He carried a small lamp,
It was dim and promised little lighting -
So he could see only what he wanted to see
He also carried a large sack like a tramp
His journey never ended but he held his oath
Pointless fruitless meaningless and so on and on...

*Some players never reach their full potential. They often start
big but by the illusion of fame they lose their way.*

"I heard you had a minor injury
But I hope you soon train with us
We have a big season ahead
We need you at your very best
Recovery takes time
But few fitness drills will make you fit
I zink this season we get major trophies
Let's get to work"

*Enza however ignored Jose's recommendation and instead
trained with his personal trainer.
This created great friction between the duo.
The worse thing was that the marquee signing Luka Ivanovic
also got injured and will be out until the next season. The results
were not good enough.*

Even the latest signing injured,
Problems in the dressing room
The bus has had started to stumble;

Few in the squad questioned his tactics -
Grumpy owners not ready to gamble
Can't afford to finish behind the plastics,
Everything ogled at sudden doom
But finding the cause means half cured.

Fans blamed the defensive style.
Media aimed for the manager's head,
Pundits claimed of awful mentality
Pressure kept on building
Banners stood out displaying brutality
Even at home games away fans started singing;
Players passion dead
Prepared the boss' sack agile

The most hated style in football
Is defensive and that's no nonsense
Newbies playing soccer games
May think football is ol' about attack
Pragmatic coaches face ol' the blame
Winning isn't enough but just attack
Best way to attack is to defend,
And counter when opponent loses the ball.

United lost two of their opening three premier league fixtures.

"I give you one more month
To fix this mess.
Else I will walk you to the door
The fans are still fuming...
Your style is snooze n bore
I have started counting
One month no more none less"

So said McCain Edwood.

The club owners set a timer.

The next match was up against Sheik Castle.

Away from home;
Heavy snow and black and black flags all around,
A very important match
United scored first -
They were in total control of the match,
Until a late equalizer...
Chants ol' around made noise sound
C'est just the beginning of the storm

Jose didn't hold back in the post match press conference.

"Some of them players they don't belong here
They belong in the championship
Or in some Bulgarian league
In terms of quality and concentration
We are no where near good enough
I don't zink I have anything to prove"

But all hope wasn't gone. Enza Gaeton was fit and ready to go.
But just before the pre match drill he got injured again.

"I said it a thousand time
And I will say it again
Your lack of commitment is your problem
I wanted you to recover with us
But you insisted to train yourself

And a run a stampede around ol' the whorehouses"

"So it's my fault?"

He replied.

"It's not your fault
It's my fault for trusting you"

There was a slight argument between Enza and Jose and it was caught on camera by some reporter. Reports spread suggesting that Jose has lost the dressing room.

More n more wounds
The medias are like vultures,
If them spotted blood -
They strangle you and surround you;
Zhe misery of another is their food.
Nothing passes through...
They have sabotaged many tenures
Suffering of another always entertain the crowds.

The upcoming fixture was up against City at the Emptihad stadium. It was a get sacked or wait for more misery kinda situation.

United got thrashed by three nil.

The away fans even brew racist comments against some of the players.

His eyes has had lost the sparkle,
Eye bags bigger than ever

Grey hairs still receding...
Voice lost its confidence.
Frustration is a desperate thing.
Driving away from prudence,
As anger blew its cover,
And the final sound of the crackle

Jose spoke to the media for one last time.

"For me there's no place for racism
I'm with the players
And always against such evils"

"Obviously a disappointing result Jose. What are your thoughts on the game?"

"There's valor in defeat
If you lose even after giving everything.
But I am sad that...
I can't say this about my team"

Jose Santos Felix has been sacked by United.

No one can predict the future,
Better to admire the past and smile
And wait till time reveals the rest of the tale.

But what could be mine,
Is not your deed.

                                        _abhin thulasidas